MW00615348

Also By Connie Wanek

SUMMER CARS

SUMMER CARS

ten stories

Connie Wanek

Connie Wanek

Will o' the Wisp Books

Published by Will o' the Wisp Books 2014

Photography by Penni Direplight

ISBN 978-0-9793128-6-1

Will o' the Wisp Books
Duluth, Minnesota
www.willothewispbooks.com

Printed in Canada

TABLE OF CONTENTS

The First Eleven Miles

When the dandelions were at their peak in mid-May, he finally tugged the tarp off his red Triumph TR6 convertible that had wintered in the big garage. This summer he would be six years older than his father was when the old man died.

Someday his son might have that exact thought, and feel the same relief, or even a sense of accomplishment, if he's honest, mingled with residual, distant grief. But his son wouldn't have this car on this perfect morning. A robin stood on the gate post with a worm still squirming in its beak, then lifted its tail to drop a white dollop onto the dark brown fence rail. Why white? What makes a robin shit white? Its eggs are blue and its breast is, of course, orange. The fence bore a long trail of similar deposits: that bird had better not shit on his car.

The robin was wary, waiting for him to disappear before venturing on, before approaching its secret nest with this ultra-fresh breakfast for the nestlings.

He could hardly wait to be out wasting gas, wasting time. Idleness in motion. Solitude and the open road, sunglasses, his hair tufts swept forward by the backward wind a convertible creates. That sad joke about how quickly one's life passes: "Zero to sixty in what seemed like ten seconds."

Think how many lovely women had sat next to him in this car! Which did he prefer, and why? This was a fit subject for early summer contemplation.

"More than ten but less than twenty," he had told

his first wife, when the car was just a few years old. It seemed a reasonable answer, but it still made her angry. Red-gold hair and freckles on her bare shoulders, Sara, small as a child, and her laugh, which ceased after the baby was born. Laughter had been the melodious soundtrack of their first days and nights.

But children bring suffering, which mothers seem to love above all else. They become infatuated with their own misery, like saints. Saint Sara. Oh, how he had prayed to her. "That said, I could have been a better man," he told his car. He had the top folded down now, tucked in, and he was about to step right over the driver's door, as he had done when he was just out of law school.

Their daughter resembled her mother so closely it was as if he had had no part in her creation. Secret thought: when Megan was 16, he was a little jealous of her boyfriends. Protectiveness, that's natural in a father. Corollary: he was furious for a good year when his son was in high school because the guy had such an easy time with the girls. The world had changed to allow relatively guilt-free, consequence-free encounters, and his son had little religious or other social scruples to overcome.

There were never seat belts in this little car. Freedom. He felt like a dog that takes half an hour to realize his collar has broken, or a horse in a field, studying an open gate. *Must be some kind of trick here.*

He'd become a lawyer for the money, back in the day. It seemed like a straightforward transaction, like, for example, the selling of indulgences by the Medieval church. Believe in Heaven? Want to go there? Haven't been good? For a fee, your passage is guaranteed.

Need a will to assure your money will survive you, still green and healthy, and end up in the right pockets? Need to sue someone rather than just shoot him? *I'm your man.* Why? *Because I know the System; I have mastered the Latin incantations with the power of life and death.* One son in every Irish family had to be sacrificed to the Church, to the priesthood. It was like tithing. Fair or not, the Law allows you to ruin someone's life. Justice was and always would be a particular point of view, like Truth. Ironically, he'd had to hire his own lawyer to represent him in the divorce.

He turned the key and the gorgeous little engine took a sip of gas. Something about its devotion made tears come to his eyes. He had had a secretary like that once, highly intelligent and completely trusting, quiet as a nun. He frowned. Too much pressure. Eventually he'd had to let her go.

This car never told him to take care of himself, to buckle up, or turn here or there. One thing he loved: the only miles on the odometer were miles he had driven, except for the first eleven. Once long ago he made up his mind to sell the car (a man can become too attached). But the impulse passed, and now he knew that he never would. He took his cell phone out of his pocket, turned it off, and laid it on the passenger seat.

The air that he and the Triumph swept through was lilac-scented, with cool and warm currents like lake water. It parted for him and closed behind him. It was as though he were passing through a crowd, smiles left and right, people stepping gracefully aside. He stopped where the driveway met the road, and there stood a wild apple tree. Petals were falling in a pink-white shower. He eased his foot off the clutch and his right foot, smart as a hand, fed the eager red horses.

Marsh Marigolds

She hated to see him suffer like this. He inched out of bed so as not to wake her, and she kept her eyes closed out of kindness. A few minutes later she heard the kitchen door squeak, then the back door click. Moonlight filled the bed on his side.

White sheets, pure pima cotton, cool to the touch. It had been suffocatingly hot this summer, bad for asthma. Things happen in threes, but sometimes we have to wait for that third thing, and waiting is misery.

He would be walking toward the creek, and though the trails had closed after the flood, he didn't need trails.

Out the window she could see their little orange VW bug parked at the curb, under the streetlight. What they would do with it this coming winter, she did not know. It had spent twenty winters in the Marshalls' big carriage-house-turned-garage, but that would no longer be possible. Would they sell it? Never. She and Jim put a good thousand miles on the car every summer, but winters mean salty roads, which meant rust. Also, it had to be admitted, the VW, lacking a heater, was poorly suited to northern Minnesota Januarys. Novembers, Decembers, Februarys also. Plus Octobers and Marches, and most Aprils.

It was, however, adorable. It was almost the orange of the summer barrels they placed around road construction, and Jim loved the attention the car attracted, especially from old hippies. People flashed the peace sign at them in the co-op parking lot. Tribal affiliation. It was the only perfect orange Beetle in town, and it had taken up very little space at the Marshalls'. They'd been so kind.

Long ago it had come to light, as they were planning to add their own garage, that the lot line between the two properties was not where they thought it was. They had assumed it was along an unused, overgrown sidewalk that disappeared into a patch of woods. But it was actually right down the middle of their vegetable garden. They'd planted corn on the neighbors' property. Jim had advanced the proposition that the Marshalls might sell them 20 feet.

"No, we'd rather keep the land intact," Mr. Marshall had said. "But how about you use our garage in the winter?" They had three cars of their own, but the beautiful old brick carriage house could have held half a dozen.

And so it had been. Every August Mary took them several pints of her raspberry jam, which they claimed to relish, and the Beetle took up winter residence in the converted Marshall carriage house. And the car went dormant till spring.

She could see the outline of the Marshalls' roof among the white pines, the biggest trees in town, saved from the lumberjacks by the lumber baron himself back in 1902 when the Tudor mansion was erected. The Marshalls had bought the property in the '40s, dirt cheap no doubt, but the times and the town had changed by then. Sadly, last January, both Rupert T. and Lillian had died within a few days of each other, and they shared a whole obituary page in the paper. He had been a founder of the Clinic, and she was in every club.

The following week a letter arrived from the law

offices of (Jim had joked) "Eagle, Seagull, Buzzard, and Loon." *Remove all personal property immediately* ("or else what?" scoffed Jim), *and surrender any and all keys.* No encroachment, no trespassing, no pumpkin tendrils crossing the lot line, no raspberry canes sending underground runners into Marshall soil, no chimney smoke drifting east into the pines, no intentions, no fond memories, no shared sorrows, no thoughts whatsoever. Jim called the lawyer whose signature was stamped at the bottom, below "Respectfully," and thanked him for the nice letter, and told him that they would remove their VW at their earliest opportunity, and that, to the best of his knowledge, they had nothing else on Marshall property. And they had never had keys.

A few days passed. A second letter came, bearing the sinister suggestion that Jim and Mary's cottage, which was long ago built to house the mansion's gardener and groom, had not been properly titled during the divestiture, back during the Great Depression, when the mansion and some of its satellite buildings and grounds had been divided and sold off.

Jim wondered if they'd have to hire their own lawyer. Mary cried all morning. They decided not to tell their grown children (who had their own lives and troubles) about the disturbing goings-on.

That evening, during the cold last week of February, they walked down the long plowed driveway of the Marshall mansion to the carriage house. A new lock gleamed against the weathered door. No one was there, but the building had been left open for them. They tried to start the bug: no go, of course. Dead battery, no doubt, and who knows what else? It was about five degrees outside, and windy, but in the calm of the carriage house it felt even colder. Their breath rose in clouds and lingered before them a good while, contemplative, before vanishing. Jim called his cousin (also named Jim) on his cell phone, and Jim and his wife Kathy helped them push the car up the icy driveway and home, then over the curb and onto the front lawn, where they had quickly and roughly shoveled a spot for it. Then they tarped it. Through their front window they could see their little beagle, Hope, barking and barking at them from her post on the living room couch. Decaf times four, finally, and talk till their eyelids felt as heavy as their hearts.

They did "retain" a lawyer, who told them what they already felt they knew: they were technically safe, but that didn't mean Big Money couldn't make their lives difficult if it wanted to. "Just because I can," said Big Money.

"However," said the lawyer, who seemed like a nice enough young man, almost a regular fellow, which was disarming, "if the Marshall heirs are planning to sell off the real estate, which they probably are, and soon, it's unlikely that they would want to pick a title fight. Purchasers don't like ambiguity in these matters. If I were you, I'd just wait. The new owners may be less aggressive."

They jumped the Beetle in May, and it started right up. Borrowed power from a fellow car, like sharing a beer, or a thermos of coffee. They took it out on a country road that followed a Lakewood township line, climbing hills a bit laboriously, then picking up speed on the descent, with all the attendant thrills of a roller coaster.

The windows were open all the way. Honest, manual cranks. And the engine, too, was a straightforward piece of engineering. This was, indeed, a People's Car. One thing they loved: the sense that they were very close to the pavement. They felt every little asphalt patch on the old county road, and they shared an intimacy with the ditches that had run so recently with clear snow melt and had now filled with marsh marigolds in bloom.

"We are only hurting ourselves," Mary suggested, "by holding fast to the things of this world, even if they are dear to us, and even if they are ours by rights."

"I hate those bastards," said Jim.

Summer Cars

Post-Hate

Every year the '68 Bonneville got bigger and Ed got smaller, except for his temper.

He had a lot of deadwood for his irascibility to burn, and some of it he had to burn twice, the way peasants make charcoal to create a more pure fire.

It kept him hot all night, this fire. It hurt like hell. Except he was convinced that he was on the right track, and he had to follow where it led. It was all he had left. Looking back, Ed could trace the first of his revelations to the Sixties, when America lost its way.

Thank God he wasn't the only one who felt like this. He never was a bumper sticker sort, especially not on the Bonneville, but he saw one on a rack at the SuperAmerica that said, "Truth Not Tolerance."

Exactly. He peeled the back off and pressed it onto the gold and silver of his car. What was eating him?

1. Hippies
2. Fags
3. Welfare bums
4. Illegals
5. The UN

You can tolerate yourself into extinction. It's dog-eat-dog. Always was, always would be. He had no idea what people were always smiling about.

In May he tugged open his garage door and pulled the canvas off the Bonneville. It was just as he had left it last October. *Semper fi.* It only had forty-one thousand, six hundred eighty-nine and three-tenths miles on it, not a scratch, 428 cubic inch V8, 390 horsepower, the full chrome package, and a radio with an antenna you pulled up out of itself. When he did that he found his right hand was shaking worse than ever.

Have you noticed all the goddamn bicycles these days? He powered down the window and stuck his left elbow out into the sun. What about those dandelions up and down the streets, like yellow smallpox?

Remember that old Coke commercial? *"I'd like to teach the world to sing in perfect harmony. I'd like to buy the world a Coke."* Bingo. He shook his head and adjusted the rear view mirror.

Next thing he knew the tires were humming on the singing bridge, and then he had crossed over the river, far below. He was rushing toward the earth again, toward solid ground.

"Dick Cheney," Betsy had reminded him more than once, "even has a gay daughter and he still loves her. You're only harming yourself. And me."

Just over the bridge was yet another Starbucks, and people were sitting at the outside tables in twos and fours, half-naked, wearing sunglasses and staring at their open laptops, or contemplating their cell phones, or else holding them to the sides of their heads. More retail, some little shops, amazing how people were coming back into the old downtown. Young mothers with kids, even, trying to rush the children along, bribing them, begging them. Everybody needed just a little more time. "You should have thought of that before you decided to have babies," he lectured.

But something about that sentiment lacked his usual conviction. The trouble is you can't be sure what you're getting into. Some kids defy you, some want your blessing. He knew, quite suddenly, where the Bonneville was taking him. It was as though a ghost had taken over the steering wheel. He pulled into the Wells Fargo Bank parking lot, near his money, and turned off the engine.

The car was on its way to see his daughter. He looked at the empty passenger seat. Betsy would know what to do if he could just see her face, one more time. Correction. She would know *how* to do all this. She would have smiled and put her soft hand on his cold one, confident in a way he had counted on from the day they met.

He felt like closing his eyes for a minute, and he laid his hands in his lap and leaned his head back. He saw her bending over the bathroom sink, putting on her brave pink lipstick, combing her wig.

Bank security approached the Bonneville a good hour later, just in time. When she couldn't rouse the old man, she called for an ambulance, and the paramedics lifted him out and onto a stretcher. Later that day, she ordered a tow truck.

Summer Cars

Building

When Mona saw the garage door open across the road that first country spring, she smiled. Tucked away in there behind his riding lawnmower, old Karl had a Mini Cooper, shiny and pristine. Clearly the Mini was a summer-only car, and she looked forward to seeing his face relax the way it did when he started a long story about machinery.

Karl brought out his Swedish flag and installed it next to the red, white, and blue on his porch, then sat down to rest on a chair just inside the garage, bathed in warm April sunlight and out of the wind. He seemed ancient to her because he wasn't well, and because she was young.

She and her partner, Suzy, had bought twenty acres across the road, a mix of woods and hayfields where they planned to build. But for the time being they lived in a '60s single-wide trailer they'd found on Craigslist. Last winter they had shifted their worldly goods to the mobile home from their house in town. Suzy named the trailer "Cat," short for catalyst, and regarded the ugly firetrap as a great spur to action. That first summer: drilled well and septic mound, two car garage, chicken coop. The first fall: foundation, rough framing, roof. Just before an early November blizzard they closed the place in. No heat or plumbing, but it was weathertight. That night they drank a whole bottle of chardonnay and were still too excited to sleep.

They did about half the work themselves, full-time

all summer till school started, as they were both strong and knew how to swing a nail gun. They drove a 1993 Volvo 240 wagon, the last year 240s were made, which they had bought when it was only seven years old, practically new. They thought Karl would approve of its nationality, at least, but he was silent on certain subjects.

He had grown up just down the road, where his father built and farmed. "He spoke Swede," Karl said, "but he kept trying to learn good English. He was mad all the time. I remember him saying, 'Oh, sure...I just learned to call it *yam*, and now they want me to call it *yelly*.'"

Karl's second wife, Linda, was still working half-time at the hospital, and nursing him as well. Sometimes Mona met her at the mailbox, and she would get quick updates on Karl. He was waiting for a kidney, and one day Linda announced, all smiles, that they'd been accepted into a special program: she would donate one of her kidneys, and he would receive one in a complicated swap involving a number of donors and recipients.

"God gave us two kidneys so we could give one away," she said confidently.

"Oh, wow," Suzy said later, when Mona shared the news. "Holy crap, she's brave."

On sunny days that first summer, Karl would back his Mini out of the garage and park it in the driveway, as though to give it fresh air. He might rinse off a little dust and dry it with a white towel, or maybe he'd just sit near it, resting on his garage chair, and watch the goings-on across the road. Linda said he approved of how hard they worked, but they never heard it from him.

"He was glad when you made them take those

trusses back," Linda told them.

"Well, they were so weathered," said Mona. "We couldn't let the lumberyard dump their rejects on us."

"That's what he said, too." Karl had been a carpenter all his life, they had heard that, but not until they read his obituary did they know he was the foreman on major construction projects in the region, the new library, the Franklin wing of the Clinic, parts of the Skywalk.

Linda and Karl took the Mini out for spins several times a week during the summer, and sometimes Karl himself drove. He'd been a dashing fellow when he was young, no doubt. His son, who came over at least once a week with the family, was a younger, stronger Karl, and the grandkids were all blond and tall and shared high cheekbones and cute Swedish noses that turned up slightly. They always waved, but they never crossed the road. Suzy blamed that on the fact—if the neighborhood grapevine was an accurate purveyor of facts—that they had started to attend services at the wife's church, the clannish Rose Hill Evangelical Lutherans.

After Karl got the new kidney, it was one thing after another across the road. Once when his son was there, they heard shouting in the garage. Not long before a final infection took hold, Linda held Karl's arm, and they crossed the center line of Zimmerman Road to see what "you girls" had accomplished. It was the second summer, and the trailer was gone, and the house was, in Mona's estimation, 86.9 percent complete, and presentable. But she was still nervous.

Coffee ("Swedish plasma"), cookies, and a tour. Karl sat down at the back door to put his shoes back on.

Sick as he was, he had insisted on taking them off as they arrived. He looked up at them, his blue eyes clear and tired, and said, "It's just beautiful. Good job."

No more than a month passed before Mona and Suzy were walking into the church for his funeral, a big turnout, and truth be told they felt a little shy. The family carefully avoided looking at them. Linda, though, embraced them at the church door, her eyes red and her face swollen. Later, the neighbor a few farms to the east said he'd heard Karl had not left a will, so Minnesota law meant everything would go to Linda, not that it was any of his business.

School started and they were swamped. One late September weekend they saw a U-Haul truck across the road, and Linda met them in the driveway. She was moving back into town, into the house where she had been living when she met Karl. She'd been renting it out for years now, but that was over and "things couldn't have worked out better."

"How are you doing?" Suzy asked, touching her arm, which turned into an embrace as Linda began to cry.

The son seemed to be in charge across the road after that. They wondered if family would be moving in—Karl had built the house, every brick, every board, so there had to be a sentimental attachment to the property. But chairs came out, a bed, a dresser, some boxes, and nothing was carried in, and eventually all that remained was the Mini sitting forlorn in the drive. After a few days it too was gone. Descendants came and plowed and shoveled, and left again, and the curtains stayed closed, the lights on timers, all winter.

The following March, on the first day that felt like spring, Mona and Suzy stopped in at Supervalu, which had once been the old Red Owl, and saw a Mini parked all by itself in the corner of the lot, out of harm's way. The car was near an ugly mountain of accumulated snow built out of the winter's blizzards, a mix of sand and salt and frozen slop that was now leaking cheerful water out of its foundation.

"That sure looks like Karl's Mini," Suzy said.

A few minutes later she spotted Linda, who was reading the nutritional label on a box of instant oatmeal, and she walked right over and put a hand on her shoulder. Linda turned. Smiled without surprise. She'd lost weight and cut her hair quite short, and was back at work full time, "doing OK."

Then they talked for a while in the cereal aisle. "He was the love of my life," Linda said, "and he's with me every day." She would never give up the Mini. "It made him smile. That's how I see him now, in the passenger seat, window down, elbow out, commenting on the gardens and fields, what people were planting, who was building and what."

When he first saw a Mini Cooper in town, she said, "He just fell for it. He ordered one from the dealership in Minneapolis to his exact specifications. He even had them deliver the car on a truck so no one would drive it north— he didn't trust them not to abuse it those first hundred and fifty miles. He was a guy who could operate any kind of heavy equipment, you know, and I often wondered what appealed to him about the Mini."

"It's like a gem, or more like solid silver," said Suzy,

"all shiny, with lots of value per square inch. It's concentrated."

"Maybe it's how well the car is engineered," offered Mona.

"Or maybe something about it reminded him of his first wife, who knows?" Linda said without rancor. "He never compared us, except to say she was impractical, which I guess meant that I was not. She was the love of his life, of course I knew that, but I did, I think, make his last years more bearable."

Shoppers were rolling their carts past, averting their eyes, as the three women with two shopping carts blocked access to the Cheerios. Something of a personal nature was going on. It wouldn't do to stare.

Nothing At All

"I can't," Mark said.

"Can't anybody?"

Mark shook his head no and filled his great-uncle's water glass from the tap at the sink. The St. Mary's hospice wing was almost new and really very nice. It smelled like off-gassing vinyl, and disinfectant, primarily alcohol. Hardly anyone had died in this bed before Uncle Ed would.

"I don't believe you."

"I have to go back to work now."

His great-uncle stiffened and turned toward the window. By Thursday he was no longer in his right mind, and sometime before noon on Friday, the heart that had beat for eighty-one years, four months, one day and a bit over seven hours, with no time off, ceased its toil.

Mark worked in the lab wrapping biceps with latex strips, slipping needles into swollen veins in the crooks of elbows, and filling glass tubes with blood. He was paged when the time came, and on his way down the maze of hallways, he called Norma, who happened to be down in St. Peter, and left a message on her cell. He called Uncle Ed's neighbor, who had asked to be notified. That was about it, except for the Cremation Society.

In his final will and testament (there had been several versions in the last few years), Uncle Ed left everything to Mark, which was stupid and, frankly, typical. Of course Norma didn't need the money, but that wasn't the issue. She was his only child, she had his eyes, his brow and thick black hair, even a bit of his temperament: No, she wanted nothing, not one thing, to remember him by. She said that with her father's conviction.

The Bonneville was his summer car, a land-yacht, Mark decided. If his great-uncle had a ghost, it sat in the driver's seat. To turn the key and start the engine was to fit his hand into the glove of the resident spirit. The Vikings would have burned the car, as they burned the vessels of the dead, setting boats adrift and watching the flames until the sea put them out.

Mark didn't have a car and didn't want one. He rode his bike and carried it into his apartment every night, across the threshold like a bride. Whatever the weather, he rode his bike. Or walked. He was a tireless walker.

Mark spent all summer, many evenings and weekends, emptying the hillside bungalow that had belonged to his great-uncle. It amused him that the siding, which looked like brick, was actually asphalt, which you could see if you looked closely. Impressions were enough for Uncle Ed. Mark cleaned like a woman, and not just any woman, but his great-aunt, Betsy, Norma's mother, who loved bleach. She'd been gone over fifteen years now.

Everything that still had some use went straight to the curb. Free, the sign said, and it was amazing what people would take. What wouldn't they take? Old shoes... gone. Stained sofa...college students? Any kind of kitchen gear seemed to be in high demand, and even old pillows and bedding spent very little time sitting out there in the morning sun. It occurred to Mark that he was earning what he had been bequeathed, and he began to feel less guilty.

There was surprisingly little of a personal nature besides old tax returns (faithfully paid) and cancelled checks, boxes of them, decades of them, an autobiography written in checks, and drafts of letters to the editor that had never been sent, full of bile. He saved Uncle Ed's driver's license, Social Security card, and limp old wallet.

But the car. Mark drove it to Moose Lake and back on the old highway, and he had to admit it was fun to waste gas and get stared at, smiled at. He could drive the car ironically, and he kept it as gleaming as his great-uncle had, laughing at himself. He took off the offensive bumper sticker, that was all. Out in the garage he found a box full of lead additive for the fuel. That alone should have given him pause.

Mark pondered how it felt to be temporarily unethical. He wondered if the Bonneville had the power to actually change him. He wasn't entirely averse to that idea. Already he had given his landlord notice: he'd be moving out and into his great-uncle's house in the fall, which he could have sold. Three bedrooms. Vast. $93,475.62, also. Norma raised her eyebrows when he showed her the passbook. After a long pause, she snapped, "Keep it."

In October Mark parked the Bonneville in the little garage off the alley, no easy matter as the car was only two feet shorter than the building and three feet narrower, just sufficient for him to squeeze out of the driver's door and side-step toward the light. The garage smelled musty, moldy, worse than the basement, and he wondered if the old wooden floor would support the car's weight one more winter. Before he pulled down the door, he took a last look: the trunk was so big it could have swallowed his bicycle, and the hood seemed as long as a football field. People always use football fields as a standard length, he thought. That's very American. He should really sell this car. He probably would.

The passenger compartment was small for such an elongated machine. What was it like? Maybe a spaceship, with cramped quarters for the astronauts, maybe like a submarine. It was easy to drive, a floating barge, quiet, the engine rumbling in the distance, power everything. At first both of his hands gripped the steering wheel, then just one hand, and finally by August he was driving with his left thumb.

One of the most interesting things to Mark was how he felt when he passed a cyclist. "There I am," he thought. "That's me."

How incredibly vulnerable bicyclists looked on the narrow side of the road! How fragile and laid bare, like dragonflies, light and darting. He knew the pounding of their hearts, and the pungency of car exhaust, and he knew the brotherhood at stoplights, men straddling their frames, touching the pavement with one toe, spitting into the gutter.

And he, with one toe, and no other exertion, surged forward from a dead stop, accelerating up inclines, insulated, at ease, his breathing steady and slow.

Freedom. But it wasn't. One felt free to choose, but that was self-delusion. Americans are obsessed by the idea of freedom, Mark knew, but it was only a word for something pure and unattainable and ultimately uncomfortable, like "truth."

Still, we live, we go on. Drinking a beer on his great-uncle's porch one gloriously mild evening in early October, staring at a shimmering rectangle, the lake glimpsed between the old Central high school and the downtown Holiday Inn, he thought about Uncle Ed's nose.

He'd seen dead people at the hospital in the line of work, but no faces as familiar as his great-uncle's. The body without its animating spirit seemed to have shrunk by a third. The bones of his face had sharpened, the nose thinner and gray-blue. Morphine had stolen any grimace. Freedom. That was the persistent abstraction gleaming in every letter to the editor Uncle Ed had composed. Was he free now?

One single thing Mark was confident about was that he knew exactly as much about the afterlife as the Pope did, no more, no less. That is to say, nothing at all.

Summer Cars

Old Pueblo

Julie relished the bland comfort of oatmeal every morning of her life. She bought quick oats at the co-op, fresh and cheap, and she gently spread the gospel of oatmeal, one of life's simple virtues, to friends and family. Over the years she had tried dolling it up with raisins, walnuts, maple syrup, even roasted pumpkin seeds, and each variant was excellent. But always she returned to the pure Spartan substance, one of the building blocks of the universe.

It had been six months since her husband had left her, not her fault, nor the fault of oatmeal. He gave her lots of money without the least complaint, which he could easily afford to do, and they heaped praise on each other as they parted ways, especially when they broke the news to the children. Just as the experts advise. In truth, the kids were grown, late twenties to mid-thirties; they were disappointed, but fine. They were busy building up their lives, filling bookcases and bedrooms.

She kept the house, of course. But she traveled, by train when practical. Here she was on April 12 in El Paso, Texas, wearing her darkest sunglasses and waiting for her dad to pick her up at the Amtrak station, a stone's throw from Juarez and all those miseries of late. It was important to keep one's problems in perspective, which a view of Juarez helped one to do.

It was Mother who drove up in—of all cars—the Shelby.

"Where's Dad?" she said after they had hugged long

and hard.

"Oh, he's playing cards."

"At ten in the morning?"

"Your hair's gone awfully gray." Julie's mother's hair was blue as a swimming pool.

They took I-10 to the Sunland Park exit at a pleasant, sedate speed, while the Mustang trembled, hyper-alive, or maybe just in need of a tune-up. The car was a pony that had gorged on oats in the barn all winter, neighing from a box stall to be let out to run. People stared at them: an old lady and a really old lady in a '60s muscle car, hugging the center line and traveling twenty miles per hour under the speed limit. Big rigs roared around them.

"Is the engine supposed to sound like that?"

"Like what, dear?"

"I don't know. Kind of screaming?"

"Hmmm. I don't hear anything."

"Are you wearing your hearing aid?"

"Of course!"

"Is that why you only have one earring in?"

"Yes it is, dear."

After they drifted onto the exit ramp, they drove up the valley, and there was Old Pueblo, where Julie had grown up. It was a sprawling adobe from territorial days, and the giant mulberry trees along the irrigation ditch were bright green where they weren't dead. In the yard, seven sun-bleached tarps speckled with grackle droppings covered seven cars, and an eighth tarp had blown against the wall. The grass was absent where the Shelby had recently been parked, and there was a dark spot of oil-soaked sand between wheel tracks.

"Oh good! Your father's home!" An EZ-Go golf cart stood under the carport, near the back door.

"Whew!" Julie's mother turned the key and the engine rumbled down to silence. Peace, as though someone had clicked off the TV, another game show no one was watching. Her mother caught Julie looking doubtfully around the yard. "I know what you're going to say, darling, and if I were you, I wouldn't bother."

The cars weren't really cars, Julie understood, as much as they were draped sculptures, or perhaps idols. Every god had a purpose: one ripened the corn, one brought back the summer sun, one gathered rain clouds, one in sickness, one in health. The Shelby for virility. "Does Dad drive at all anymore?"

"You should see him out there with your brother, lifting up the tarps and planning long road trips. Peas in a pod."

Julie tugged her bag out of the trunk. She remembered the time they tried to start the red Corvette with the white dished-out sides, she and her brother. Gas? Check. Oil? Check. Battery? It was probably the battery. Their parents were off at a university dinner that evening, and it was all very hush-hush and unsuccessful. And then she thought of the day the silver Jaguar arrived, a spring day like this one, windy and almost summer-hot.

Two men pulled up in a crummy pickup pulling the car on a trailer. Her father was waiting in the yard, all eagerness and nerves, as the men backed in, and started to ease the car down the loading ramp in neutral. Suddenly it began to get away from them, and they shouted in alarmed Spanish and leaped out of the path of the Jaguar.

For a moment it had looked like disaster, but the car rolled majestically into place, gleaming in every curve like a relic from the Art Deco era. *Gracias a Dios! De nada, de nada.*

She remembered her father lifting up the hood and staring into the abyss. He was a historian with immaculate hands and narrow shoulders; her mother was the superior mechanic. Her father maintained that driving the car, while it would have been gratifying, was not strictly necessary. "This car just breaks my heart," he sighed, weeks after its delivery.

"Because it won't run?" Julie had asked.

"No, because it's so perfectly lovely," he said, "and because I own it. Doesn't it seem as if no one should own it? It's like a waterfall. No one should own a waterfall."

He always made mild fun of Julie's penchant for Toyota Corollas, because they weren't "interesting."

"They run," was Julie's stock answer.

And now he was hobbling out through the back door, using two canes.

"Daddy! What happened?"

"Nothing, nothing. Come here!" He leaned on her shoulders then, instead of the canes, and she felt the sharp bones in his back. Was he crying? Oh no, it seemed like he might be.

"Stay here with us," he whispered into her hair. "We need you."

Julie's heart sank even as it filled. This was going to be complicated.

Our Bus...Well, One of Our Buses.

The weather here in Duluth doesn't give an inch. No one's going to negotiate his way out of November, not even if he's Mr. Fred Dudderar, Esq. Appearances demand that we all corral the ethereal maple leaves and stuff them into plastic bags. This also gives us the illusion of accomplishment, which is central to our lives.

Fall is the season to dream longer in the dark, as bears do. Imagine giving birth while you're asleep and waking to find a baby! I guess that used to happen to women. Remember those big families? Four and six and eight? The Swiss family, the Robinsons, for instance? Robinson: not a particularly Swiss name, a reference to Defoe? Injuries healed on their island, and they lived in hope and faith, despite the pirates. Meanwhile, life in a treehouse was delightful.

When I was fifteen my father bought a retired school bus, with little thought, apparently, as to why it had retired. This vehicle was to be our motorhome, our growling bear, our treehouse with tires, our family sailboat. My mother, a tireless inventor, set to work on the interior. My mother: quick, powerful, smart. My mother: an army of one. Tackle, not tag. True grit. Six kids were a temporary, part-time job.

Storage, upholstery, built-in bunks and fold-up table, stove/fridge/toilet/laundry/heat. Sun, moon, wind, and flickering shadows. No AC though, of course. Her magic had limits.

My father took his place behind the wheel, his cold pipe clenched in his teeth, as we set out from Las Cruces on our summer vacation. We crossed the Jornada del Muerto in safety, and my father's face was calm as he ordered everyone to bed. He was determined to drive deeper and deeper into the cool of the desert night. Perhaps he'd pull over somewhere to rest, tossing his anchor into the sand for an hour, then waking suddenly to see the stars had shifted, and pulling up the rope hand over hand, an hour lost. I may have roused then, hearing the engine start again, and tiptoed forward to share his solitude, because I remember his profile by the light of the dashboard, his private firmament.

The Sacramento Mountains were a saint's trial, and our old bus climbed them by means of faith, love, and diesel fuel. The engine was hot. So hot. At last we reached the summit, at a maximum speed of twenty-five miles per hour, and began the descent. Then the smoky smell came from the brakes.

The plan, such as it was: drive north to Mother's Wisconsin before the June heat did us all in. We'd already had a week of 100+ degrees F. in the Mesilla Valley. As we left New Mexico for West Texas, about twenty miles shy of Amarillo—that is to say, nowhere—the old bus, the island, the Ark, the treehouse, the bear, the bus-shaped planet slowed down and came to a stop on the shoulder of the Interstate highway, while the world rushed on.

My father looked pale by the morning light, like a man with a bad ticker. The long night had drained away his tan. Anger never showed on him, but sadness did, weariness did. He pulled the heavy chrome lever to open the bus door and descended the tall steel steps. He looked back west. Maybe this trip wasn't such a good idea. He looked east into the summer glare, the big rigs and assorted cars rushing away in an endless herd, tugging on his restlessness. A pickup truck stopped and a Texan wondered, did we need help? Man, woman, six children, dead bus. Yes, in fact, we did. We were forty years too early for the cell phone.

A tow truck pulled the bus into Amarillo: "yellow" in Spanish. We were deposited in a big, ugly, hot parking lot for broken semis. Boredom set in, but isn't that Amarillo all over? Utter stasis. Several painful days passed before my father accepted at last the mechanic's diagnosis. The bus was, indeed, terminal.

Here's what happened then: Dad bought a brand-new genuine Winnebago, manufactured in Wisconsin, and we transferred clothes, food, bodies, maps, books, and dreams into the Solution.

Forty-something years down the road I look back at that summer differently, knowing more about the grief my parents must have felt, stranded in a glittering, broken-glass, chalky, burnt, oil-scented Purgatory. Hell was to stay there. My mother's mother sat on her porch, waiting for us, loving and patient, in Heaven, aka, Wisconsin. Hafiz says, "We don't need sugar, flour, or rice or anything else. We just want to see our dear ones."

Now I know how much work it was to earn the money to buy a motorhome brand-new off the lot, and also how bitter it was to leave behind all the careful work poured into bunks and cabinets and a built-in dust bin, all the sewing required to cover those boxy foam rubber cushions with green canvas and welted seams, creating places for six children to sit, eat, read, and complain.

Now I see those several days in Amarillo as the opposite of boredom. For parents it was a time of crisis, of intense spiritual taxation, when all of life is seen whole and found futile, when the cure becomes suddenly obvious and irrefutable: spend the hoarded money and keep moving.

Finally, I know that there is no foolishness or failure that, given time, doesn't look like a sound course of action again, one worth repeating, because this next time, with a different big yellow bargain bus, it just might work.

The Death of a Car

We had driven the narrow forest road to Alden Lake that spring at least a dozen times before I happened to notice the car—its rusted, bullet-ridden body—about thirty feet into the pines. We stopped to investigate. This was county land, we thought, although we weren't sure where the lines fell. It could belong to Minnesota Power, or even to one of the big lumber companies.

Didn't seem to matter: it was just "the woods," and people had hunted grouse and deer around here forever. Now that they were talking about a season on wolves, this would be a likely area for that, too, judging by the copious, hair-packed wolf scat along this lonely stretch.

We had the camera with us, and we parted branches for each other as we pressed through a thicket. Underfoot lay about six inches of soft pine duff, or so it felt. No doubt the ground was still frozen below that. It was only late April, and this was twenty miles north of town, where frost goes deep and stays long. Upon reaching the car, we saw no obvious damage from a long-ago collision; it had died a natural death (all death is natural). However, at some point, a tree had fallen on it from behind and then rotted away, judging by the big dent in the roof, right down the middle.

Men with shotguns and rifles like to shoot signs, bottles and cans, and, obviously, an old car if there happened to be one, while they waited for the right animal to materialize in the cross-hairs.

Alders had sprouted up through the floorboards in

the front, directly through the tattered rubber mats (still there). Dogwood, too, had spread into the interior, leafless still, but bright spring red. The dash and steering wheel were essentially intact, and two pedals still offered themselves up stiffly to a phantom foot.

The seats were rusted springs sans upholstery. The driver's door was missing, the windshield broken out, the hood gone. There was the engine, though, sunk down onto the ground, massive cast iron covered with lustrous green moss.

Debris and leaf litter, pine needles, red shell casings, Old Milwaukee beer cans, and a Forties-era canister vacuum cleaner about the size and shape of a fire extinguisher—all this and more were heaped in and around the car. It was not so much an object as a landscape. Looking at our photos later, I realized that the exterior had once been painted burgundy.

A plate on the frame read "Chrysler Corp Detroit Mich." Vehicle No. 31920033. Stamped into the metal: 816107. The body style? A Google search suggested the car was likely a circa 1939 Plymouth, ten years older than my husband but significantly younger than our parents.

I tried to think who might have had the money for a new car at the end of the Great Depression. What hands held the wheel? Who checked and changed the oil, or a flat tire? I knew cars could be loved (and hated) and it's possible that whoever bought this car new might still be alive, might remember it, might recall the chest-expanding sense of ownership as he drove it home for the first time. Unlikely, though. Less likely all the time.

Born into a world already rushing toward another

war was this foundling in the woods.

Now at rest in such peaceful surroundings, though something about deep pine shade feels gloomy, slightly sinister, and then—all those bullet holes. What spider silk touched my cheek as I pressed through the balsam thicket, back toward our waiting pickup truck? What kept that oak leaf attached all winter long, only to fall at this very moment, brushing my shoulder?

Summer Cars

He Was Saving It

Why do people narrow as they age? They harden, too, beginning with the arteries around their hearts. He felt that happening to him, and he fought against it. He thought of this effort as exercise, perhaps as intellectual yoga, and lately it took this form:

He drove slowly through neighborhoods where the political yard signs were offensive to him. Just seeing the wrong names and irrational assertions made his blood pressure rise. This fall the presidential election made such unconciliatory neighborhoods easy to find.

He tried to distance himself from his irritation, to contain it. To neutralize it chemically, by adding a base if it was acid, an acid if it was base. The final step in this exercise was to argue from the opposing point of view.

Let's say he passed the brick church on Arrowhead Road that had hundreds of identical white crosses on the lawn, each one signifying an aborted fetus. Normally he would dismiss such blatant self-righteousness, such a simplified view of complex circumstances. Often he would allow himself the small fantasy of pulling up all the crosses and throwing them into the dumpster below the parking lot, or right through the stained glass window: the very window that depicted a human being enduring terrible cruelty—torture in fact at the hands of fellow human beings—the agony of which this church fetishized.

Right. This was the challenge: try to see this as a caring place where people didn't intend to be vicious and point fingers at everyone but themselves. Rather, people at this church hoped to return the whole world to a place where they felt secure, where the rules were good rules, and young people didn't get tattoos or infections from tongue studs or use the "F" word as though it were simply punctuation. This final challenge included the fantasy of stepping up to the pulpit on a Sunday morning, looking out at expectant faces, and not saying anything offensive.

So far he hadn't made much progress.

It was on one such excursion into enemy territory that he saw, of all things, a Volvo P-1800S parked at the end of a driveway with a For Sale sign taped inside the windshield.

He was driving a Volvo, an S-60 sedan, which he pulled directly over to the curb. Every single car he had ever bought, used or new, had been a Volvo, even though his was a family of Norwegians.

He got out and walked slowly around the little car, late '60s, he judged, then peered into the window and saw that the odometer, if it was correct, read 48,254. Someone had been holding on to this car for a very long time without driving it much. Not a speck of rust, either.

His face suddenly felt hot, and his body filled with excitement and desire such that he began to think he was slightly delirious. The word that came to him was "swoon." "My God," he thought, "I'm swooning!" He could buy this car with mere money.

It was like the old Catholic notion of indulgences: you could purchase your ticket into Heaven. Even more amazing, you could shorten the years in Purgatory for your beloved, and no one could argue with the necessity of that.

The wind gusted, and a small tornado of maple

leaves spun up the sidewalk. Serious weather was on its way from the Dakotas. This was to be the last warm day.

It was at exactly this time of year, ages ago, that his good friend in high school, Patrick Heaney, had gotten his driver's license, and his father who was a locally famous heart surgeon, responsible for several technical innovations that had transformed prognoses for hundreds of patients, presented Pat with his first car, a brand-new Volvo P-1800, pale blue in color. How casually the son had received it, and how carelessly he drove it.

Look back. Memories compress, collapse like spent stars into impossibly dense matter, then explode.

Pat was an only child, given everything twice over, and to shake himself free he joined the Army right out of high school and died quickly in Viet Nam.

Down the block some idiot was stalking around his yard in the wild wind, leaves spinning, twirling, leaves stripped from whole branches in an instant, the yards flooded with red and gold leaves racing from hedge to hedge. This nut case had his leaf blower out, trying to herd the leaves and bag them, but they were evasive, they teased him, they had other plans.

What ever happened to Pat's P-1800, or any of his stuff? No clue.

Part two of that story actually took place before part one. Patrick had gotten his girlfriend, Lily, pregnant, and she confessed to her parents, who told his parents, who paid for Lily's plane ticket to Hawaii where abortion had recently become legal. Problem solved. Money could do that, too. Money, what powers it had, and how it bent people to its will. Lily came back to school slender, and sweet as ever, by all appearances.

After they buried their son, had the Heaneys ever thought about Lily's child? Or Lily?

But what is this thing we share and call "life?" Say the baby had been born, and instead of a handsome Einstein, they'd raised a sly bully, a cheat, someone who, for example, scammed old people out of all their savings for a living. Try as you will to do what's best, to insulate yourself and those you love from harm, life can go terribly wrong.

Or right. That's possible, too. He'd worked hard, saved, been honest, tried to be moral. He had also been incredibly lucky, healthy, long good marriage with no cheating, two terrific kids grown up and moderately happy.

He laid his hand on the roof of the P-1800S, which was warm from the sun. It was a feminine little car, immaculate, pure white with a blue interior, two seats, a coupe. Delicate headlights and a grill that looked friendly but shy, yes Swedish, white-blond with a summer tan, slender with curves. The tail fins were rounded and reminded him of trout.

The car looked small enough to pick up, to carry over a threshold. It barely came up to his elbow. He would have to fold himself up to fit behind the wheel, so it seemed, to make a child of himself to drive it.

He heard someone speaking to him in the wind. "This car," it was a man's voice, "I was saving it." He turned, but there was no one on the sidewalk, no one in the yard. He was alone on a wild fall day, except all the leaves were suddenly turning into birds, small yellow warblers fluttering up, whisked away in an instant.

He tugged out his cell phone and dialed the number on the For Sale sign. He would buy this car today. Every new mile it traveled would be his. He would take perfect care of it. As long as he lived, this car would be his.

Summer Cars

Paperwork

It was an imperfect situation, one that couldn't be leveraged into concessions, and anyway, Falk was in pain.

His hand shook a little and his "F" began to look more like an "R". The paperwork seemed to take forever, and he had to shake his head no, again and again, and still he wasn't sure what all he'd signed in the end. If he were ten years younger he would have driven a harder bargain.

Oddly, though, he began to feel compassion for this young salesman. Thief River was too small a town to hold a grudge, or to start one, and much too small for any man to be an actual thief, not for long.

"You're not your father," Falk said as the keys to his new Fusion were ceremonially presented.

The salesman had not yet mastered his face. He seemed to drop through a menu of possible expressions before he clicked on rueful. "We all miss Dad."

Then Falk handed over the keys to his Ford pickup. That hurt. But with the cabin sold and no boat to tow and nothing to haul, the truck no longer justified its appetite for gas. The Falks were leaving Minnesota for good in favor of their winter home on a golf course in Texas.

"We're right next to a sand trap," Falk liked to say, weary of his own joke, "at 66 Money Pit Boulevard. Come visit us." But really, it had to be this way, such were the limitations that age had imposed, especially on his wife. He had always taken care of her, and he always would.

What he found interesting was the stock response from people up here to "no more winter." Variations on the theme of "you lucky bastard," especially the proximity to the golf course, a game that bored Falk stiff.

The truck was like new, though it was an '03, with only 50,648 summer miles and an engine that had seldom been tested by circumstances there on Otter Lake, 16.2 highway miles north of city limits and pavement right up to their sandy driveway. The Falk garage was bigger than the cabin, and heated by a big propane wall furnace. He'd had a TV out there mounted up above the workbench, like a trophy moose head, with a greasy remote at the ready. He could watch the Twins and even the Vikings when the two of them had stayed at the lake deep enough into the autumn, which was the best time of all up north. Quiet during the weeks, and no bugs after the first hard frost, and the fishing picked up in the lengthening shadows. Fall was the season for last chances.

People complained about losing the light, the short deep blue days, but Falk felt himself sharpen in the cold. Something about the glare and heat of Texas made his head buzz and his eyes ache.

He'd always worked his trucks hard, but this one had had an easy life. Like a big black bear, it had hibernated all winter in the shelter of the garage, sleeping off the fruitful summer days. The bed of the Ford had only a handful of shallow scratches. Falk felt younger in a truck, more in control. He liked the sound of a powerful engine when he turned the key, enlisting hundreds of horses and maybe a few stubborn mules.

Well, some lucky SOB would get the deal of a lifetime on this Ford, and it was only recently that Falk found he didn't mind giving up an advantage instead of taking it. Not quite true. Of course he minded. But that's what pain does to a man. Make it stop, *now*, he said to a pill.

The Fusion was just a car, and its engine sounded whiny and high-pitched, as though its voice hadn't changed yet. But she liked it, color first (some kind of green), and it was not a "fall in, climb out" sports car which she nixed. It was respectable, practical, anonymous, like a B student in Civics. "I don't mind being bored by a car," she had told the salesman, who had an exaggerated smile for everything she said. He helped her in and out, and used his good looks against her.

"I wish I had a better number for you, Sir," he had said to Falk when he'd given him the truck's trade-in value. Always "Mister Falk." Always "Sir." Then the salesman had worn his most apologetic expression (the one, no doubt, that his wife knew so well) when he came out with that little scrawl on a scrap of note paper.

But the Falks were leaving. No incentive for this young guy to treat them fair and square in hopes of future business.

Well, what's done is done, he thought as they accelerated toward I-35 south. The Fusion would serve them for the duration. He adjusted the rear view mirror where the pines had become a dark, ragged horizon, nothing more. What do I hate most about this, he wondered. His wife was already asleep, her head resting on the little purple pillow she always traveled with, her face swollen from the meds.

He was sick of giving up everything he loved. That seemed the essence of aging. You're supposed to be a good sport, he knew, to shake hands when you say farewell to what you were, sitting up high in the finest truck Ford ever built.

"They are all like us," his wife told people about their neighbors in Texas. "All from somewhere up north, making the most of the time they have left."

As he sped up the long hill out of Thief River, Falk made the only resolution that could ease his mind. "You haven't seen the last of me, little town," he said. "By God or the Devil, I'll be back."

"One good thing about Texas," she told people, "is it's still in the Midwestern time zone. You wouldn't believe all the trouble that saves."

Connie Wanek lives north of Duluth, Minnesota, where in May, when the weather settles, summer cars begin to appear on country roads and city streets. She is the author of three books of poetry, most recently *On Speaking Terms*, published in 2010 by Copper Canyon Press. www.conniewanek.com.